Compliments of
Topsail Township
Friends of the Library

PLEASE JOIN

Night
and the
Candlemaker

For Gabriele — W. S.
For Nicola, Mam, Dad and family — S. B.

Barefoot Books
37 West 17th Street
4th Floor East
New York, New York 10011

This book was typeset in Palatino Bold 18 on 26 point leading
The illustrations were prepared in acrylics / alkyds on primed watercolor paper

Graphic design by Judy Linard, England
Color separation by Printex, Italy
Printed and bound in Singapore by Tien Wah Press (Pte.) Ltd.

This book has been printed on 100% acid-free paper

1 3 5 7 9 8 6 4 2

U.S. Cataloging-in-Publication Data (Library of Congress Standards)

Somary, Wolfgang.
   Night and the candlemaker / written by Wolfgang Somary ; illustrated by Simon Bartram. —1st ed.
[32]p. : col. ill. ;   cm.
Summary: As the candlemaker works, Night comes to whisper fearful threats and to bring darkness.
ISBN 1-84148-137-8
1. Night — Fiction. 2. Sleep — Fiction. I. Bartram, Simon, ill. II. Title.
   [E] —dc21   2000   AC   CIP

Night
and the
Candlemaker

written by Wolfgang Somary

illustrated by Simon Bartram

walk
the way of wonder...
Barefoot Books

All the world was sleeping.

Just one person was awake, and he was all alone. Just one light flickered on the windowsill of his simple workshop. He was the candlemaker.

Night crept through the town toward the candlemaker's workshop.

Without a sound, Night slid under the door, then rose up behind the candlemaker as he dipped a long, thin reed into a vat of warm beeswax.

"Your work is useless!"
hissed Night. "My darkness
can overpower whatever amount
of light you may kindle during your
brief life span."
The candlemaker nodded and dipped
another reed into the wax.

Night pressed on. "You may light a candle, but my friend the wind will snuff it out!"

"I shall protect it with a glass lantern,"
replied the candlemaker. "Then the
wind will become my friend
and diffuse the light."

After awhile, Night whispered, "I can bring down snow to cover your light!"

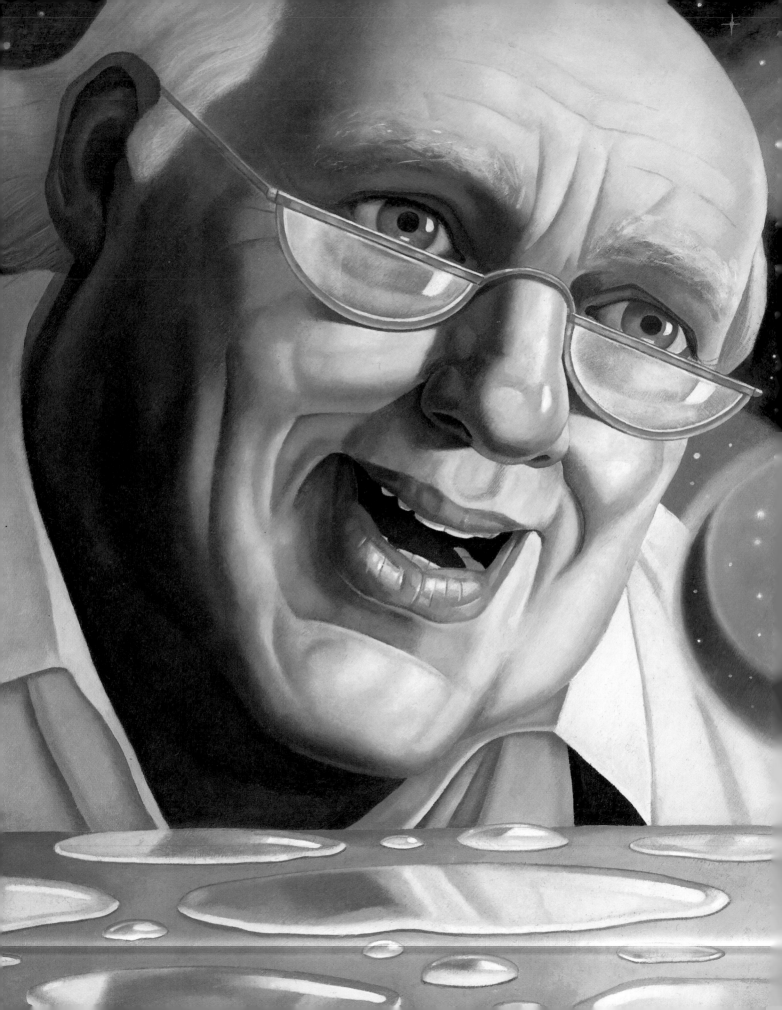

The candlemaker replied, "And the light will melt it and mingle with the water, all the more to be reflected and seen."

The room was warm with the smell of beeswax.
The candlemaker dipped another reed, while Night,
fidgeting with irritation, mumbled, "Even then,
you will never find the path that leads to
the hills of hope, because my blackness
is longer than your lantern beam."

"I shall see enough to take one step at a time," replied the candlemaker, "and surely I shall be on the right path, because I walk with the light and the light walks with me."

After a long moment of silence, Night mumbled, "Don't you think it's time to catch some sleep?"
"No," replied the candlemaker. "Tomorrow people will come to buy candles."

"Tomorrow?" asked Night softly. "What tomorrow? Are you sure there will be a tomorrow?"

The candlemaker had nothing to say. He just carried on working. The candle in the window had nearly burned out. He lit another with the dying flame and let it blaze high, and another, and another, so that even in their dreams, the people would know that he was attending to his task.

"What are you doing?"
demanded Night angrily.

"Making tomorrow," replied the candlemaker.

walk
the way of wonder...
Barefoot Books

The barefoot child symbolizes the human being who is in harmony with the natural world and moves freely across boundaries of many kinds. Barefoot Books explores this image with a range of high-quality picture books for children of all ages. We work with artists, writers and storytellers from many cultures, focusing on themes that encourage independence of spirit, promote understanding and acceptance of different traditions, and foster a life-long love of learning.
www.barefoot-books.com